TO END ALL WEEPING

Robert Lorenzi

author HOUSE®

AuthorHouse™
1663 Liberty Drive
Bloomington, IN 47403
www.authorhouse.com
Phone: 1-800-839-8640

First published by AuthorHouse 8/18/2011

ISBN: 978-1-4634-0106-1 (e)
ISBN: 978-1-4634-0107-8 (dj)
ISBN: 978-1-4634-0108-5 (sc)

Library of Congress Control Number: 2011908067

Printed in the United States of America

To the memory of Robert Lorenzi, Jr.

TABLE OF CONTENTS

TO END ALL WEEPING

Here the weeping puts an end to weeping.
- Dante, translated by Mark Musa

The Storm of the Century
January 6, 1998

He was encased in ice.

On his 70th birthday, Danny Donati awoke in the midst of an ice storm. It had been sleeting in Maine for three days, and it still hadn't stopped. Yesterday seemed the worst.

The electricity had gone off while he slept.

Shivering, wrapped in his blanket, Danny stumbled to the kitchen. He automatically flicked the light switch.

"Stupid ass," he mumbled. "You know, idiot," he said aloud to himself, "when there's no electricity, the light switch doesn't work." Often sarcastic with himself, Danny was alone long enough to scold himself for his stupidities.

He grabbed a log and shoved it into the wood-burning stove. When the ice storm had begun, Danny hauled logs into his cottage.

His cottage on Damariscotta Lake in Lincoln County, Maine, was on the far end, literally ten feet from the water. The window at that end of the cottage gave him a view of the main part of the 13-mile lake. Today there was an accretion of ice that blocked the view.

This cabin on a Maine lake was an idyllic setting in the spring, summer and fall -especially the fall. However, the winters were long, dark, cold and often stormy. But Danny had never experienced the severity of a storm such as this one. Large accumulations of snow were not unusual. It seemed once it snowed, the snow never went away until spring.

"I have everything I need," Danny often reminded himself, and he mumbled that to himself now. He always kept a massive supply of canned food, spring water, and logs for the stove. And books - he had enough books to satisfy his voracious reading, he estimated, for six years. He felt secure in his independence, like Thoreau in his cabin at Walden Pond.

After his wife Bea died five years ago, Danny abruptly resigned his professorship at a community college in New Jersey and ran away from his past life to Maine to exile himself.

Bea's suffering from ovarian cancer almost killed Danny, too. His love for Bea was unending. The stress of her suffering and death caused him angina pain that led to open-heart surgery - triple bypass.

"You would have had a heart attack," the cardiologist had told him.

Danny ran away from something else: his only son's drug addiction. Bea's dying words: "I'm free. I'm sorry to leave you with Billy."

Billy had become a heroin addict at 17. Bea and Danny became codependent resulting in their finances bordering on bankruptcy. But Danny was always able to pick up extra teaching work to make ends meet though they were forced to sell their house.

After Bea's death, Danny lost all of his energy.

"I'm through with you, Billy." He withdrew all of his savings and with half, opened a savings account for Billy. By himself, Danny could lead a Spartan life on Damariscotta Lake.

"I have everything I need," he reminded himself. Danny, living this isolated life, often talked to himself. "I have the logs."

He noticed the electric kitchen clock had stopped at 2:48. Though he knew his cabinets were filled with canned goods, he opened each to satisfy his security.

"I even have a couple bottles of wine," he reminded himself. He tried the phone but it was dead.

He slipped on a sweater and trousers and rummaged through a kitchen drawer to find batteries for his radio.

"It's estimated that 75% of the state is without power. This ice storm of '98 has crippled most of the state with electric lines and telephone lines down.

"The storm has been raging since Saturday with the worst accumulation yesterday of almost an inch and a quarter of frozen rain."

The commentator went on about emergency crews, aid shelters, and warnings to stay indoors.

"I'm glad I have everything I need in this place," Danny repeated.

The cottage had been one big room when Danny bought it 12 years ago, but Danny added partitions to create a kitchen and two bedrooms. He and Bea came to Maine every summer since they purchased the place. Some summers, Billy and one of his girlfriends showed up. And on two occasions, Danny's sister Gerri and her husband visited. They were happy days except when Billy had to find heroin - when he became agitated and angry. Billy never stayed long.

Bea and Danny always found their own happiness in each other. Before the "Billy problem," Danny had once told Bea, "It's scary. We've been so happy and had such good luck, it frightens me."

Bea laughed. "We'll just have to live with all this joy."

The unhappiness in their lives had been Bea's three miscarriages. Bea had Billy when she was 40. She devoted her life to raising him. Billy was a wonderful child - good-humored, lively, intelligent.

Danny and Bea never knew what went wrong. "God didn't want us to have this child," Danny told Bea. "He warned us three times."

"There has never been as severe a natural disaster as this," Danny heard the reporter say.

"Indeed, people are calling it the storm of the century."

Conversations with Bea

His love for Bea was undying - so much so that five years after her death, he still spoke to her - and amazingly she responded - if not in words, in thoughts. He still knew what Bea was thinking.

Danny had met Bea after he completed his Bachelor's degree. After knowing each other for one year, they married. Even though she had gone to work immediately after high school, she was a voracious reader. She enjoyed reading classical literature, but also had knowledge of American literature - Dan and Bea had much in common.

Beatrice Porter, born in 1932 in Paterson, New Jersey, blonde, blue-eyed, often referred to Danny as her "dark Italian Gothic villain who kidnapped her." Danny, also from Paterson, born of immigrants, referred to Bea as his "American," rolling the 'R' and accenting the last syllable to give it the Italian pronunciation.

Danny was a friend of Bea's cousin. They met at a party given by Bea's cousin. Soon they realized that they were in love.

And they still are.

After heating his instant coffee on the wood stove, Danny sat in his rocker for his morning conversation with Bea. He never started his day any other way.

"You should see the weather here, Bea. Unbelievable. Not snow. Freezing rain. The cottage is a cake of ice. Worst storm ever.

I can't see out the window to see the lake. But I have everything I need.

"Billy, wherever he is, is not in Maine, so he's not out in this storm."

There was a long hesitation as Danny thought of Billy, hoping he was with friends and not living on the street. He hadn't heard from Billy in over a year.

"I tried, Bea. I gave him enough money to survive for a year. I paid his apartment a year in advance. But I had to leave. If I didn't, I would probably be dead by now.

"Remember how naive we were in the beginning? When his friend Jason forced Billy to tell us, we assumed that all problems could be solved. We packed him off to rehab. We were surprised at how long we had to wait to receive approval from our insurance company. We thought we could just put him in immediately. Three hours later, the receptionist congratulated us upon Billy's acceptance. Congratulations? We were amazed. Congratulations because our son is an addict and the insurance decided to accept him into a facility for four days. Of course, there would be a re-evaluation to see if he could stay longer, we were told. Of course, it was up to the insurance company. Not the doctor? Of course, the doctor will have his input. Input? Of course!

"Were we naive or what? The gracious insurance allowed him eight days even though the doctor recommended two months.

"But that was it, we figured. He's detoxed, all better, back to normal. Within 48 hours he was back on the street looking for dope. And we became codependent, feeding him money. I began to feel like an addict myself. It didn't take us long to realize there were problems that could not be solved. The realization of unsolvable problems is a rude awakening. We never believed there were problems that couldn't be solved."

Bea's thoughts came through to Danny: an assurance that Billy was all right where he was now.

"Can you really tell these things, Bea?"

Danny wiped the lone tear that trickled down his cheek. He laughed.

"Then you know about this storm, too! Maybe you can tell me when the electricity is coming back on - and the telephone."

No response.

"I love you, Bea."

The Storm of the Century

Danny tried to open the cottage door, but it wouldn't give. He mustered all of the weight of his 160-pound body and rammed himself against the door once, twice, three times.

He had to sit now and control his heavy breathing. There was a slight throbbing in his chest. He sat back, relaxed all his limbs, and took deep breaths. He heard his heart pounding throughout the cottage.

Danny always had an irrational rage to him at the smallest things that he could not accomplish immediately.

"Your Italian temper," Bea used to say.

Little things like not finding a comb, or accidentally spilling some drops of coffee, or breaking a shoe lace -these irrelevancies would make him fume and let forth a stream of verbal rage. He was so creative in the curses that Bea often laughed at his foolishness, which made him all the angrier.

Now he was trying to control himself about the door. Doctors told him that he had to control his anger to avoid the stress that affected his heart. Through the physical exertion and his inability to open the door ("the fucking door"), Danny had brought on the throbbing.

Danny meditated, trying to think of pleasant events in his life. There were many - all with Bea and young Billy: Their vacation on Cape Cod when Billy was three years old, he remembered now.

The image of holding Billy on the beach on a windy day came

to mind. Looking out to the ocean, the white caps thundering in on this blustery day - what happiness - pure joy - Danny felt that day with his son in his arms. All was right with the world. "God's in His heaven / All's right with the world."

The wind was riffling the weeds at the edge of the beach. Billy laughed at the movement of the tall grass.

"Rasmussins," Danny told him.

Billy looked bewildered.

"Rasmussins. They're little creatures that run through the tall grass."

Billy buried his face on Danny's shoulder.

"Me no like Rasmussins."

The memory calmed Danny. It brought a smile. His breathing had returned to normal.

He tried to look out the windows but they were all caked with ice. He tried to see the nearby cabin of Paulie and Fran, the young couple next door. He wondered if Paulie got out. Paulie checked on Danny regularly, so Danny assumed Paulie, too, was stuck inside.

"Maybe they just stayed in bed late," thought Danny. "No need for young lovers to get up on a day like this."

He picked up his Hawthorne book and resigned himself to a warm wood stove, a comfortable chair, and a day of reading his favorite American author. He was reading all the stories that he hadn't read.

He stuffed the stove with more fire wood. He still had a good supply. "After all," he thought, "this storm won't last forever." In truth, it wasn't as bad as yesterday, but it was still sleeting.

"I'm sure Paulie and Fran have everything they need," Danny said aloud. He laughed, imagining the two young lovers in their bed.

Fran had been married before, but her husband neglected her in so many ways. Johnny was a skilled welder. His work took him to different parts of Maine and New Hampshire. He would be gone several days at a time -sometimes a week, or ten days.

Fran worked as a waitress at the Back Street Landing in downtown Damariscotta. Johnny rarely left her any money. One winter before a work assignment, Johnny was supposed to chop firewood. He forgot.

Fran had known Paulie since high school. He delivered bread to the local restaurants and often timed his deliveries to be done by noon so that he could have lunch at the Landing. He always sat where Fran would be his waitress.

They always made easy conversation with each other. Usually the Landing did not have a large lunch crowd, so Fran was able to talk to Paulie. Paulie was disappointed if the restaurant was crowded because Fran wouldn't be able to talk to him.

Paulie always admired Fran and couldn't believe she married Johnny. Paulie knew what a womanizer Johnny was, and he was sure Johnny was an alcoholic.. What kind of life could Fran have? Paulie was sensitive to her moods.

The day Johnny left, forgetting the firewood, Paulie noticed that Fran was upset. When he asked her what was wrong, she said, "Nothing," but burst into tears.

That same evening, when Fran came home, there were neatly piled logs. She couldn't believe that Johnny came back to chop the wood. He didn't. It was Paulie.

It wasn't long after that Paulie visited Fran regularly. Johnny had been gone a week when Danny noticed that Paulie dragged two wooden horses, the kind the police use to block a road, from the garage to block the driveway. He had moved in with Fran.

"Holy shit!" was Danny's comment when he heard Johnny's truck pull up. Johnny got out and threw the horses out of the way.

Danny saw Paulie on the porch with a shotgun.

Obviously, the conversation was not pleasant. But Paulie calmly told Johnny he had to leave. He didn't give a reason.. .the gun seemed reason enough.

Danny was ready to call the police.

"Don't be in the woods during hunting season! Remember, this is my house!" Johnny shouted as he jumped in his truck, spun his wheels in the gravel, and sped away.

That was two years ago. After a messy divorce (which included threats of murder and mayhem from both sides), Fran and Paulie were married. Their love reminded Danny of his love for Bea. Just as Danny and Bea would be together through all eternity, so would Paulie and Fran. Danny just knew that.

Danny liked Johnny, and Fran loved him once upon a time. Johnny's excessive drinking and absences slowly alienated Fran from him. She didn't mind his having to go away to make his living. It was the lack of communication that bothered her. He never called; he often arrived days later than he was supposed to.

He made good money, but Fran never saw any of it. She subsisted on the money she earned waitressing. She hurt, but never complained. But the firewood instance was too much for her to bear.

After Johnny was kicked out, he visited Danny.

"What happened, Dan?"

Danny was momentarily speechless. How could this friendly guy be so insensitive?

Eventually, Danny found words: "Don't you know?"

"But it was so sudden. She never complained."

"Maybe she should have. But didn't you sense her unhappiness?"

"No." Johnny shook his head.

"How many women have you had since your marriage?"

"I don't know. How could she know? I was on the road. I needed to be satisfied. How could she know about any of them?"

"She knew." Danny was amazed at Johnny's - what? - stupidity, naivete, self-centeredness. "Why would you come home days later? Even I understood that."

"But I'm young. I need to be satisfied."

"So does she," Danny said. And there was a long silence.

"But over the damned firewood," Johnny eventually said.

"Over the damned firewood," Danny repeated. There was nothing else to tell Johnny. He simply refused to understand.

"You know I'm going to kill them - at least him," Johnny said.

"Over the damned firewood?"

"No - you know," Johnny was like a child who lost a toy. He did not understand Danny's sarcasm.

"Now listen," said Danny. "You're not going to kill anyone. Just recognize that you've lost her. Pick up and get yourself a new life. The one with her is gone."

Johnny shook his head like a dog not understanding its master's command.

He got up to leave, obviously not fulfilled by this conversation.

"Bye, Dan. I will kill them, though."

"Get that out of your head." But Johnny had already stepped out the door.

Danny had some sleepless nights. He often thought he heard a car coming up the dirt road in the middle of the night. But time passed. The divorce was final, and Johnny disappeared.

Danny had continued his reading of Hawthorne. He nodded off and was awakened by pounding and scratching on his door.

"What is it? Who is it?" Danny shouted through the door.

"Are you all right, Dan?" It was Paulie. Danny tried to push the door open, but couldn't.

"I'll have it open in a minute," Paulie said. He was banging and scraping and pulling. Finally, the door cracked open sending ice flying like miniature stars.

And there was Paulie, pick ax in hand, in the swirling wind, all 260 pounds of him, his face red from the merciless sleet matching his red beard now sprinkled with ice. His tall, massive body stepped into the cottage. The wind helped push him into the cottage. The wind had no specific direction. It was probably coming in across the frozen lake, but as it hit the trees and the cottage, it swirled pushing the sleet in different directions.

"An infernal storm," Paulie grunted, shaking ice from his hood and from his beaver fur coat.

Danny inspected the door. The ice was more than two inches thick on the door, on the jamb, and, Danny assumed, completely around the cottage. He forced the door shut.

"Let me heat the coffee."

"Never saw anything like it," Paulie said. He pulled off his hood and opened his coat. "Need to get warm," he said, removing his gloves and rubbing his hands over the wood stove.

"You should have a ski mask," Danny said, putting the coffee pot on the wood stove.

"Never had one."

"Thanks for going through all this trouble."

"Had to. Worried about you. Phones are out." Characteristically, Paulie expressed himself in brief non-sentences.

"Appreciate it." Paulie's habit was contagious.

"Needs?"

"I have everything I need." Danny pointed to the stacked firewood. "Brought it in when they predicted the storm. Have food, water." Danny pulled out one of his bottles of wine from the refrigerator. "This will warm you up."

Paulie smiled his approval. His white teeth broke up the constant red of his face, his beard, and his brash hair.

"He has to have Scottish blood in him," thought Danny. "He would make a perfect Macduff, a man of action, powerful, sensitive." His masculine frame defied the tenderness that Danny had seen him convey to Fran. Paulie was muscular, very little body fat, a hunter. During hunting season he was off to the woods. There was something basic about his joy of returning home to Fran, carrying the evening meal with him - in his truck if it was a deer. It was more fulfilling than driving the delivery truck.

They drank the wine, sipped it slowly. Danny offered some food, but Paulie declined. Fran would be preparing lunch.

"When is it supposed to stop?" Danny asked.

"Don't know. No radio."

After the wine and friendly small talk, Paulie dressed for the storm.

"Wait," said Danny. "I want to look at the lake."

He began putting on boots and the warmest clothing he could find. He wasn't as prepared for the outdoors as Paulie was.

"Still there," grunted Paulie.

Danny trudged through the ice encrusted snow with difficulty. He leaned on Paulie's arm.

"Easy, Dan. Go back inside?" "I have to see the lake."

Damariscotta Lake was more like a sheet of glass than frozen water. The small island off to the right of Danny's property looked as if someone had decorated the trees with tinsel. As he looked across the lake, Danny noticed branches of apparently dead trees poking their way through the ice. At such a distance they looked like human heads popping through the ice. The vision sent a deeper chill through Danny. He had never felt so cold - to think of humans frozen into the lake!

The larger island, a good distance off to the left-center, could hardly be seen through the pounding sleet.

It was all a wondrous sight. Danny held his body stiff against the wind. The sleet stung his face.

"I've never seen it as beautiful and as frightening in all this violence of nature," Danny said.

"Still wish it would stop," said Paulie.

"Isn't it beautiful, Bea?" Danny whispered.

"What?"

"Nothing," Danny said to Paulie. "Let's get inside."

When he looked back at his cottage, it was a block of ice. The outlines of the building could not be discerned. Danny thought of the blocks of ice delivered to his grandfather's ice box. His cottage seemed ready to be shoved into a gigantic ice box made for some monstrous mythological beast.

Paulie made sure Danny didn't fall as they returned to the cottage. Danny thanked Paulie again for his concern.

"Be here every day till the phones work. Call you then."

Danny stood by his open door and watched Paulie crunch his way up the small hill of a driveway that led from Danny's cottage to his.

The wind seemed to pick Paulie up and swirl him up the hill as he returned to Fran.

Billy

With the early darkness setting in, Danny thought of Billy.

Danny remembered back in New Jersey.

It was after the third rehab that Billy told Danny, "The only thing I got out of rehab is that I learned to shoot up. Before rehab I only sniffed."

"Why can't you make it work?"

"You don't understand. Just give me sixty dollars." By now Billy was 20 and all pretensions were gone. He used to lie about his need for money. Now he simply demanded it.

"But I don't have it. Here's twenty."

"Fuck you. That's not enough."

"Well, fuck you, that's all I have. You're sending me to the poor house."

"Come on, go to the bank. I know you have money stored away."

"I'm not going to the bank."

Billy had been drinking.

"Okay, then. I'll have to shoplift, probably get arrested. Is that what you want?"

"I don't even care."

"That's just it, son of a bitch. You don't care about me. You never cared."

"If I didn't care, I wouldn't be here.

"Shit." He punched the wall. "Mom!"

"What is it?" Bea shouted from upstairs. "What was that noise?"

"You got any money?"

"No."

"You bitch."

"That's your mother you're talking to."

"I don't give a fuck. I need money."

"Here's twenty dollars. Now get the fuck out of here."

It was after this incident that Danny decided to get Billy an apartment.

When Billy was sober, Danny could reason with him.

"It's apparent," Danny told him at a calmer time, "that we can't live in the same house."

Billy nodded in agreement.

"Everyone - counselors, other patients at NA Meetings - says that I have to cut off all ties with you - leave you alone - not support your habit."

"So, I live on the street?"

"No. I won't abandon you. I'll give you a place to live and food, but other than that, I'm through with you."

"I'll get a job," Billy said. Billy's jobs lasted until the first paycheck. After that, he never showed up for work again.

"How do I get around?" Billy asked.

"I'll drive you to work."

That's not what Billy meant.

"What about when I have to go to the store?"

"Walk. I'll take you. We'll figure that out."

That still wasn't what Billy meant.

After a pause, Danny said, "Look, I'm not driving you to Camden or Philadelphia. You will have to find your own way."

Billy said nothing. His look was impassive.

"As far as your drugs are concerned, I'm through with you, Billy."

The Storm of the Century

January 7,1998

The sleet came at intervals, but it still came. There still was no electricity. Danny tried the phone - still dead.

He decided he had to do something with the food in the freezer. He plopped the ground meat in a pan and put it on the wood stove.

"I hope Paulie comes over. This will be too much for me to eat."

He filled garbage bags with the remaining food. He was able to force his door open with a strong shoulder shove. He had to leave the bags on the ground. With the encrusted cottage, there was nowhere to hang the bags.

He tried to hammer a nail in the ice but it merely cracked the ice, and the nail would not hold.

So he had no choice but to tie the bags and leave them on the ground. He did not have the energy to carry the bags through the sleet and ice to the storage bin around the back of the house.

"If animals get at it, so be it. The food will only go bad in the freezer," he spoke aloud as was his habit. "In the bin, the mice will only get at it anyway."

The work exhausted him.

"No damned energy," he mumbled.

He picked up the phone to call Paulie before he remembered the phone was dead.

"Stupid ass."

He wished Paulie would arrive so that he could share the food. He went back to his book, but Hawthorne, with all his secret sin, was depressing. He found a Mark Twain book.

"I need to laugh a bit."

While he read, the cottage took on the smell of the cooked meat. It was a pleasant smell, and it made Danny hungry. The smell reminded him of Bea's Sunday dinners. She was a pretty good cook for an American. Before they were married she bought some Italian cookbooks. She was smart. She learned fast.

He remembered sitting at the dining table with his in-laws, his parents, Gerri and her husband. There were bottles of white and red wines, an antipasto, loaves of bread on the table. Carrying a large, steaming bowl of macaroni, Bea came from the kitchen into the dining room. Over all the food smells, Danny could remember the smell of the steaks cooking while everyone was enjoying the pasta. Bea always made extra sauce. The steaks sizzled. Bea would jump up in time to catch the steaks at the perfect moment. Danny always wondered how she did that.

While everyone was finishing the pasta, Bea would - again with perfect timing - arrive at the table with the steaks.

Paulie did arrive to share the food.

"Can't begin to get the delivery truck out," said Paulie. "Everything's got to be shut down anyway."

They ate.

"What's in the bags?" Paulie asked.

"Frozen food. I guess animals will get to it."

"Maybe, unless they're frozen or afraid to come out of their holes."

Paulie thought a minute. "Take them to my place," he said. "Put them on my balcony upstairs. Safer."

"It's too much trouble for you," said Danny. "This thing's got to be over soon. The electricity will come on today or tomorrow. It has to stop. I've got an appointment up on the hill on the 11th. What's the date today?"

"Seventh. I'll take the food. Bring you some tomorrow."

"You don't have to bring some tomorrow," said Danny. "I have canned food - soup -vegetables. I have all I need. I just don't want to put you to the trouble of carrying those bags."

"No trouble."

They heard three sharp blasts from a siren.

"What the hell!" Paulie jumped to his feet and pushed open the door.

He could see an emergency vehicle up at the end of the normally dirt road that led to their two cottages. A hooded creature that Paulie assumed was human was trudging down the incline.

Paulie hastily threw on his coat. The hood was walking into Paulie's driveway.

"Hey!" Paulie called to it (him?).

The hood stopped.

"You folks need help?"

The hood changed direction and walked to Danny's cottage.

A face emerged.

"They set up a shelter at the high school," the man told Paulie. "Anybody want to go?"

"No. Thanks. We're okay."

The hooded face looked at Danny who was standing in his doorway. "Got heat and food? Water?"

"I have everything I need," Danny shouted above the swirling wind.

"Ya sure?"

"Uh-yuh. Thanks for coming by," said Danny. "When's it supposed to clear?" Danny asked.

"By Friday."

Paulie grunted his thanks.

The hooded face turned and tramped back up the incline and became a creature again. The creature turned and waved and disappeared into the vehicle and drove away, red lights flashing.

"Good news. I'll make my appointment on the hill," said Danny once they got back into the house.

Paulie found his hat, bundled himself. "I'll take the bags," he said.

Danny stood by the door as Paulie hoisted the two bags, one over each shoulder, as if they were weightless.

As he began his trek, Paulie turned, "Dan." Danny thrust his chin as if to say "what?"

"Dan," Paulie said, "forget about the appointment on the hill." And once again he turned and rode the swirling wind.

Conversations with Bea

Mark Twain didn't make Danny laugh. It was time to talk to Bea.

"Remember Nantucket?

"We were staying at Provincetown with Lonnie, Jane, Carol, and Steve and decided to take a day trip to Nantucket. The kids were younger than five.

"Billy was fascinated by the buoys bobbing as we neared the island. He pulled another of his 'me no likes.' 'Me no likes bou-ees,' he laughed running around the deck.

"When we got to Nantucket, Steve, reading a bulletin board, discovered a house we could rent for the night. So our day trip turned into an overnight trip.

"We stopped for breakfast and ordered blueberry pancakes. Some memories are so clear. Steve's son Michael saw the pancakes and asked, 'What are the little blue things in them?'

"It's nice to remember the happy days.

"In the middle of the night I heard Steve jump up and run outside. He thought the cat crying in the street was his baby daughter.

"In those days you could stop a teenage girl on the street and ask if she would baby sit - which we did so that we could go to a restaurant.

"Times have certainly changed."

Tears came to Danny's eye when he thought of little Billy

because the momentary memories of good times were always interrupted by the more recent bad times.

"He was intelligent enough to make anything of his life.

"Now you never know who's the drug addict.

"Remember the night I told Billy not to go out? He had been drinking.

"You'll get into an accident," I told him.

"He went anyway. About an hour later the phone rang.

"Dad, I'm parked in the Presidential Arms Apartments parking lot. The car's wrecked. Come and get me.'

"He had rammed the back of another car and drove away. His car barely made it to the large parking lot, where Billy hoped to hide it.

"I drove through the lot with my windows open, looking for his car. I heard him shout. He emerged from the shadows, jumped in the car.

"Get the hell out of here."

"But, of course, someone had seen Billy's license plate. It was the first time he lost his license.

"My prophetic ability did not make me proud.

"I told you to stay home"

"Well, I didn't and it's too late now to think about"

"You had better do some serious thinking. Your life is going to shit. I've always tried to tell you that life is not a joke.'

"I don't want to talk about it.'

"Well, I do. Think of what you're doing.'

"There's only one thing I'm thinking about - it's who to call for a ride. We're half way to Philly. Why don't you drive me?'

"I knew it was no use reasoning with him, but I'd be damned if I would drive him. I drove home.

"Get one of your so-called friends to drive you,' I said to him as I got out of the car. 'I'm through with you, Billy.'

"Why is it, Bea, that we always come back to Billy? No matter what we start talking about, it always winds up with Billy.

"Billy, Billy, Billy - I'm so glad I'm through with you."

The Storm of the Century
January 8, 1998

The sleet had stopped but the wind blew strong across the lake.

The ice would not melt.

The radio:

"Power is slowly being restored to parts of the state. It is estimated that 68% of the state is without power - mostly north of Augusta. Up north, 35% of Portland is still without electricity."

Danny clicked off the radio. The pile of firewood was dwindling.

He found an old ski mask at the top of the closet. Dressing to face the cold, Danny could find only one glove.

Before he went outside, he tested the phone again - still dead.

When he got to the outside pile of firewood, the logs were frozen together. He could not separate them. His ungloved hand immediately went numb when he tried to pull a log off the pile.

He looked up the driveway. The swirly wind created a white haze, like looking through gauze. He thought he might walk up the long road to the mailbox. The road went slightly uphill all the way to the end, about a mile. Then there was the road beyond the mailbox.

"Friday I'll have to cross that road and climb the hill beyond," thought Danny. "No matter what the weather," he said aloud.

He began to walk to the mailbox. When he passed Paulie and Fran's cottage, he slipped on the ice and fell to his knees. His hands hit the snow to keep him from falling on his face. There was the shock of biting cold in his ungloved hand. The wind continued to swirl. Even with the ski mask his face felt frozen.

Struggling to his feet, he slipped again. On the second attempt, he was upright again. Wolf, Paulie's dog, began barking.

Danny struggled for ten more yards. Then a gust of wind from behind caused him to lose his balance. He tried to take another step and pitched forward on his hands and knees again. He became dizzy. Each time he tried to get up, he slipped on the ice. He breathed heavily. He thought he might not be able to get up.

Suddenly Paulie's strong arms pulled Danny up by the armpits.

"Where the hell do you think you're going?"

Danny grunted. His eyes were glazed. He couldn't speak.

Fran came running out. Her heavy parka hid her athletic figure. Her big, brown eyes looked out from the hood. Her usually tanned face was red from the wind and ice.

Paulie's strength got them back to the cottage. He had to half drag Danny back. Paulie sat Danny in the chair next to the wood stove. Danny shook. He tried to pull the ski mask off but couldn't. Paulie pulled it off along with Danny's wet coat and wrapped the old man in a blanket.

Fran was heating water.

"Some warm tea?" She was speaking to Paulie. Danny seemed incapable of thought.

Fran, the swimmer in summer, ice skater in winter, loosened her parka. She was as tall as Paulie. Her hands moved busily through the cabinets searching for tea.

Danny held up his frozen hand. Paulie threw a towel on the wood stove and then wrapped the heated towel around Danny's hand. Paulie threw two more logs into the stove.

"Runnin' low. Need more by tomorrow."

"Stuck together." Danny's voice was a mere whisper. His chest hurt. "What?"

"Stuck." He could get only one word out this time. "What's stuck?" "Logs."

Paulie found a crow bar under the sink where he knew Danny kept his tools. Within minutes Paulie brought an armful of logs into the cottage. Fran brought Danny the tea. He had trouble holding the cup. Fran lifted the cup to his lips. Fran's hands were strong. They were strong, useful hands. Her long fingers wrapped around the cup. Danny welcomed the hot liquid. He felt the warmth travel through his body. After the tea, Danny went to bed. Still shivering, he awoke the next morning. The kitchen light was on and the phone was ringing.

But the freezing rain had been falling again - all night.

Danny's Dreams

His dreams were hazy and sporadic. As with all dreams, they blended into one another illogically.

Danny was on a cliff. He looked down at four tombstones. He couldn't see them clearly, but miraculously flew off the cliff, like Icarus with waxed wings, and landed in front of the tombstones. One had his name on it, and it was right next to Bea's. There were also Fran and Paulie's next to each other.

Then Danny was back on the cliff. Johnny was dancing to a fast fiddling song. He was at the very edge of the cliff, but remained suspended and rushed right back onto the cliff.

There was a child wailing behind Danny. As Danny turned, he saw five-year-old Billy crying.

"You left me! You left me!" the crying child shouted at Danny. "No, you left us!" Danny told the child.

As Danny reached for him, Billy's face changed into Johnny's face.

Suddenly, Danny was back in his cottage cooking the meat he had removed from the freezer. As he looked into the pan to turn the meat, Danny saw Johnny's face smiling at him.

Gerri

January 9,1998

His sister Gerri was on the phone.

"Danny, Danny, I was so worried," she sounded relieved. "I heard about the storm -and then I couldn't get through to you for days."

"The phones were down - no electricity either."

"Move back to New Jersey so I don't have to worry about you living in that wild country, in that small cottage. What are you doing for heat?"

"I have a wood stove."

"That's not enough. Get back here to civilization where there's central heating."

"The stove heats the whole place."

"That's because you live in a place no bigger than a broom closet. Come back here. I have two empty bedrooms."

"Ger, I like it here."

"Yeah, freezing your ass all winter, fighting flies and mosquitoes in summer."

"Better than fighting the air pollution and traffic in Jersey."

"You're hopeless."

Gerri decided to change the subject.

"The people who bought your old house painted it an atrocious lime green."

She went on about the changes since Danny left. He realized

she hadn't changed the subject at all. Everything was designed to get him to return to New Jersey. He realized how good it was to have a loving sister. She made him miss her, but he didn't miss New Jersey. He loved Gerri, but he also loved Maine.

"How's Billy? Have you heard from him?" Danny finally asked.

There was a profound silence.

"I know. I know. It's okay. I'm finally through with Billy."

"That's good," said Gerri softly, gently, sympathetically. "You have to accept what's happened."

There were tears in Danny's eyes. There were tears in Gerri's voice.

"Now, Danny, you take care of yourself. Do you have enough food? Don't go out until it's safe." Gerri had the motherly instinct.

"Don't worry. My young friend Paulie is here to help me if I need him." He wanted to reassure her so that she wouldn't worry too much.

"I'll call you tomorrow," she said. "Don't go outside."

He didn't want to tell her about his appointment. Why make her worry?

Johnny

Danny heard a car. A few minutes later he heard a pop that he thought was the car backfiring.

"Who would be driving a car here in this weather?" he thought.

Then he heard someone pushing on his frozen door. In burst Johnny, with ice flying all around him. Johnny slammed the door shut and stood like a washed-out forlorn Frank Sinatra, staring at Danny.

Johnny's hair was soaked with ice and snow. His face had the remnants of the cold, but that ruddiness was fading under the body's stronger urge to have the blood drain from his face.

"What the hell!" Danny said. "What are you doing driving around in this ice storm?" And where you're not wanted - Danny thought.

"He took a shot at me," Johnny managed to say in a choking voice.

"Shot? Who?"

"That bastard Paulie. He told me not to come around anymore. He had his rifle. He tried to kill me."

Danny guided Johnny to a chair. "Calm down."

"Calm down! How can I calm down when someone tried to kill me?" He looked around the room. For what? Danny didn't have a gun.

"Look here, Johnny," Danny said, "he didn't try to kill you.

You know Paulie's a good shot. He wouldn't have missed you. He just scared you."

Johnny thought about it. He stared at the floor. He kept flexing his hands. "I'll call the police," he finally said.

"Johnny," Danny said, "it's over. It's over between you and Fran. The best is to go away."

"He's keeping me from my own house."

"You left, Johnny. The divorce - "

"Bullshit."

"Get a lawyer. Do whatever you have to do legally. It's over. What are you doing back here?"

Johnny stared. The color - now from rage - was returning to his face. His eyes were glazed. He had been drinking.

"It's not over. It's not over till I kill both of them."

Danny felt a pain shoot through his chest at the shock of Johnny's words. He couldn't speak right away, but now Danny wanted to call the police.

When he caught his breath, Danny tried to reason with Johnny.

"Don't even think that. You have to face reality. You're not going to kill anyone. You're a young man with your life ahead of you. Put the past behind."

After hesitating, Danny then asked, "Why'd you come back? It's been - how long - years?"

"I decided I want her back. The bitch I was with - I couldn't stand her anymore. I decided I want Fran back. And if I can't have her, I'll kill her. I'll kill him either way."

"You're being irrational. Forget this life you had. It's over. Move on to another life."

"You don't know me." Johnny stormed out.

Danny rushed to the phone to call Paulie.

When Paulie answered, Danny heard the car start.

"He's leaving," Paulie said.

"He threatened to kill you," Danny said.

"Never happen."

"But..."

"Don't worry," Paulie said, hanging up the phone.

Bea
January 10

"I had a sleepless night. Stupid dreams.

"Johnny's back. Every sound in the night had me thinking it was him. But I couldn't see out the window because the ice is still not melted. And what am I gonna do besides call the police? I fear the worst."

He waited for Bea's advice to come to him.

"I know. I'm always worrying about something. It used to be Billy, but I'm through worrying about him now.

"You're right - I can't do anything about Johnny - and I never could do anything about Billy. I still think I should call the police about the death threats.

"Maybe I helped Billy too much in the wrong direction. Like the time I gave in and drove him to get his heroin. He was nodding out. I was driving around the back streets of Philadelphia missing turns because he would pass out. I had to smack him, punch him, to keep him awake. I finally told him I was going to drive back home.

"By some miracle he woke up as I passed the drug set. He went into a house and emerged with his stuff. When he tried to inject, he nodded out. I drove him home with the needle in his arm, the dope still not injected.

"By then, he was living in his apartment. When we got there, I pulled out the needle. He was living with one of his girlfriends

-I can't remember which - so I got her to help me wake him enough to get him to his feet and the two of us, with his arms over our shoulders, got him inside. And I gave her the needle with the dope in it - ready to be injected - so that when he woke up, he wouldn't have to risk his life again by going to the Philadelphia slums.

"Wrong. Wrong. So wrong the things I did for Billy.

"I couldn't do the tough love. I tried, but I always felt so sorry for him I would give him money.

"But that was the only time I ever drove him to get the stuff.

"Now I still think of him, but I'm through worrying. I'm finally through with Billy."

January 11

Appointment day arrived. Danny arose at daylight, dressed himself as warmly as possible. If Paulie wasn't ready as promised, Danny was determined to go alone.

As he emerged from his cottage. Danny saw two police cars at Paulie's. He trudged over. Two policemen were accompanying a handcuffed Johnny.

The scene immediately registered in Danny's mind. Crunching through the ice that covered the snow, Danny made his way to Johnny.

"Stand back!" shouted one of the policemen. "Stand back, Danny!" the other echoed. Danny recognized that cop.

"Nick," he said, "what's going on?"

"Never mind," said the cop that Danny did not know. "Who are you?"

"He lives next door," Nick explained.

Danny knew what happened. He lunged forward and grabbed Johnny's coat.

"You finally did it. Why, John, why?" Danny was punching Johnny's chest. "Get away from me, old man," said Johnny.

"Did he finally do it?" Danny asked Nick. Weeping, Danny fell to his knees.

Nick turned Johnny over to the two other policemen. He grabbed the weak, old man firmly by the arm and led him back to the cottage. Danny, trying to turn to talk to Johnny, tripped twice on the way, but Nick's grasp kept Danny from flopping into the ice-encrusted snow. The wind whipped wickedly at their backs and propelled Danny's frail body forward.

Nick got Danny inside the cottage.

"Now, Dan, you have to sit here. Detectives will be here to question you. Stay put." "He finally did it," Danny said sobbing with certainty. "The detectives will be here soon." "Tell me what happened." "I can't Dan. I'm not supposed to." "Please, Nick, I have to know." "You know, Dan. You know."

"Both?"

"Yes."

"How? Why?"

"You know why, Dan."

"How?"

"I'm not supposed to say anything."

"C'mon, Nick. Just tell me."

Nick hesitated. "He shot them both while they slept. Shot them in their own bed."

Danny covered his eyes with his hands. He dropped his hands and looked at Nick. "It was once Johnny's bed."

Nick began to leave.

"Thanks, Nick."

"Okay. I wasn't supposed to say anything, so don't make me look bad."

Danny nodded. "I won't."

"Just stay put," Nick said as he left.

Danny sat staring at nothing. Slowly the tears welled up in his eyes.

"Paulie and Fran - dead," he muttered. 'Dead. Why, John? Why? What have you accomplished?"

He sat silently weeping. Suddenly, he became alert. "The appointment."

He bolted out the door. An ambulance had arrived and Nick was observing the medics as they were wheeling one of the bodies out. The other two cops were watching Johnny, who was now in the back seat of one of the patrol cars.

Danny was determined to keep the appointment, but he knew

if he were seen that he would be stopped. There was a rock wall - rocks piled up about a century ago - as a boundary to his property. "Good fences make good neighbors." The wall came up to his hips. He struggled over the wall and began crawling. He was on a thin sheet of ice that covered the snow. His elbows, as he pulled himself forward, cracked the ice. He was flat on his stomach and thrust himself forward like a soldier on a secret attack mission. His layered clothing protected him from the cold.

Danny made slow progress. Every few feet he would peek over the wall. The medics were still busy. Danny knew he had to get beyond the policemen's sight before the detectives arrived and came looking for him. He figured he had plenty of time because he would not be the primary concern of the detectives. The crime scene would be of more interest to them. But he hoped Nick wouldn't go back to the cottage.

With great determination Danny crawled - elbows, knees, feet. The wet was beginning to seep through his clothing.

He heard a vehicle pass him up the mile-long road. When he peeked over the wall, he saw that the ambulance had gone. The police were still there, apparently awaiting the detectives who may have been coming from Augusta. He also noticed that in a few more feet he would be beyond Paulie and Fran's house and out of sight of the police. The house would block their sight.

Struggling a few more feet, Danny pulled himself to the top of the rock wall and rolled over it. Still prone, he needed to catch his breath before trying to stand. Working up to his hands and knees, he pulled himself up with his left arm hugging the wall. He was up on his left foot, but his right foot slipped on the ice and he wound up on his hands and knees again. He, this time, thrust both of his arms over the wall and was able to pull himself upright. He felt dizzy. He leaned on a tree to catch his breath and let the dizziness pass.

He remembered that Paulie had promised to go with him. How he could use Paulie's help now. But the thought of Paulie brought tears. The merciless wind froze the tears on his face.

Danny's walk up the inclined road was painful. He was now walking against the wind, slightly uphill. His feet broke through the ice crust and plunged into the snow. He made better progress when he walked in the tire tracks made by the vehicles, but they were slippery and caused him to stumble.

But he made it to the end of the road and crossed the country highway. Now he had to climb a hill to get to the appointment. The task seemed insurmountable, but as far as Danny was concerned, there was no choice.

As he slipped, step after step, he often had to throw out his hands as he fell. But he was undaunted.

The wind in his face burned and he was having difficulty breathing. Then the angina pain began. Breathing became more difficult, and the pain spread from his chest downward to his left ribs and upward to his neck.

He had remembered to put his bottle of angina pills (Nitrostat) in his mitten. Flopping to his knees, he gently pulled off his left glove and found the small vial. He had to take off his right mitten to remove the cap. His shaking, freezing left hand poured four pills into his right hand. He thrust them under his tongue and shakily screwed the cap on, throwing the bottle back in his left mitten. Both gloves now were wet and afforded him little protection from the cold.

It took him three attempts to get to his feet. The wind was relentless. He had to close his eyes to let the dizziness pass. The chest pain was subsiding.

He continued his trek. The wind forced him to pause every few yards. The steepness of the hill and the vicious wind were both working against Danny, but the top of the hill was in sight.

Then the pain returned - more violent than ever. He removed his gloves, but found that the Nitrostat pills came out of the bottle. The cap was not screwed on tight. The remnants of the pills were in his wet glove. Many of them had disintegrated. He found one that he thrust under his tongue, but the others were liquid. He licked the white spots inside the mitten.

This time the pain did not subside. With all his remaining strength, Danny struggled to his feet. He staggered the remaining distance to the tombstone on the top of the hill.

Dizzy and in pain, Danny fell to his knees. He wrapped his arms around the tombstone that read:

William A. Donati September 8,1974 January 11,1997

"I'm through with you, Billy. I'm finally through with you."

The pain shot through the back of Danny's skull. His eyes rolled as the whole world spun around him. He fell backward into the snow and ice. In the overcast of clouds and sleet, Danny saw the beautiful stars.

Nick found him encased in ice. Danny's tears formed a visor around his eyes for the cold wind had frozen them on his face.

ADDRESS UNKNOWN

On November 1,2030, Cass Wilder received a letter from his local post office, as everyone in the United States did, saying that as of January 1, 2031, there would no longer be local post offices. The letter explained that since 99% of all mail is now sent via email, there is no longer a need for local post offices. For the "rare instance" that a "paper letter" is sent, there will be available for the "convenience" of all "post office patrons" a state post office located in the state capital city. Also, for the "convenience" of those who did not have computers, there would be an office located at the county seat. The monthly cost would be $300 to have a post office registration number entered into the computer. All computers would also have a registration number so that only those with matching numbers could use that computer.

Cass' number was 10004743-216. The letter said that his computer is the same number. Cass was confused because he had no computer.

When Cass called the telephone number in the letter to ask questions, he was told that it was assumed everyone had a computer, but since he did not, the male voice told him to go to Houlton, the county seat, and all would be taken care of. He gave Cass the address.

Houlton was still too far for Cass to drive, and the $300 a month would be too expensive.

Cass Wilder, 90 years old, lived in Big 20, Aroostook County, Maine. Big 20, now, has fewer than 20 people in this village that is in the northern most part of Maine. There are no state highways. Logging roads are the only roads in Big 20.

Cass never had a computer, never used email, even when he worked years ago for The Maine Professional Guides Association, where he became a legend. He was the most famous hunting and fishing guide, leading his clients into the Maine wilderness, to areas where people were not permitted to travel without a guide.

One of many legendary stories about Cass occurred in 1969. Two flower-children adult men decided they would go observe the behavior of bears on their own. They got lost in the woods.

Cass figured out where they were. He knew amateurs would take the trail that seemed the safest - though it was not. Within hours Cass tracked them down. By merely noticing a few footstep impressions along the trail, Cass knew he was on the right track. Everyone thought Cass had a sixth sense, but he knew he did not. It was logic and a familiarity, since childhood, with the wilderness. His father, Dirk Wilder, had taken Cass hunting and fishing in the wilderness since Cass turned six years old.

Now Cass lived with Sniper, the last of his many hunting dogs, deep in the woods of Big 20. For 56 years he had lived with his wife Isabel, but she died thirty years ago. Cass still thought of her every day.

Cass no longer hunted. He had memories of Isabel and memories of hunting. His arthritis hobbled him for the last 18 years, and it got worse each year in the cold climate of northern Maine. He refused to move to a warmer climate - to Florida, where his son lived. He told himself that he could not live anywhere else.

Once known for his exceptional eyesight, Cass had noticed his vision failing him for the last decade. He saw no need to see an eye doctor because he could still see well enough to drive the few miles to purchase his necessities. But he drove only in daylight.

He lived frugally on his small pension and social security checks which he had directly deposited into the bank.

No one lived near enough to Cass to call a neighbor. He did not care. He preferred being alone with his thoughts of Isabel - and with Sniper, whom he talked to regularly.

Now this letter!

Cass received very little mail - only utility bills and an

occasional letter from his 68-year-old son, who lived with his family in Key Largo.

"My boy never took to the wilderness - hated hunting and fishing - hated this place he called God forsaken - headed south when he turned twenty-one," Cass said to Sniper often-every time he thought of "young Bert." Bert always kept in touch. He now owned a hardware store in Key Largo and apparently had a happy life.

But this letter! The state capital! Augusta? Houlton?

"Do they think we live in Rhode Island?" Cass asked Sniper. He estimated a trip to Augusta would take at least eight hours. Eight? Nine? Maybe more!

Cass knew he would never receive another letter. What did that mean? Electric bill?

"I won't be able to pay it because I'll never receive it. Maybe I can pay by telephone. But what about the phone bill?"

Water?

"We have our own well, Sniper, from a nearby stream."

Tax bill?

"Local grocery store - they accept checks."

IRS?

"Never will pay again because I'll never be able to send my tax form, which I'll never be able to get." Cass laughed and petted Sniper.

Bert's letters?

"I'll never hear from him again."

Cass mailed all his bills to the end of 2030.

"That's that," he said.

Sniper shook his head in agreement.

As the months of 2031 went by, the phone company called him about his bill. Cass said he would pay it at the local grocery store.

"No, sir," the female voice replied. "It must be paid by email."

"I don't have email," said Cass.

"Well, go to Houlton. There's an office..."

"Can't drive to Houlton," Cass interrupted

"Well," said the voice, "I'm sure you can find someone to drive. A neighbor?"

"I don't have any neighbors." He slammed the receiver.

To negotiate the $300 a month, Cass called Pay Them Off, Inc., of Houlton.

"But I only have two or three bills to pay a month," said Cass.

"We can handle that," the male voice said.

"But at $300 a month?"

"Sure thing!"

"How about a lower rate?"

"Three hundred dollars a month is a low rate."

Cass hung up.

Cass tried the local grocery store where he had often paid his electric bill.

"We can't do that anymore," the clerk said.

Cass sought out the owner, Ebenezer Root, whom Cass had known for about 40 years.

"Sorry, Cass, it's now against the law. People have to use their own email or the email of certified agents like Pay Them Off."

"But I can't afford $300 a month to pay my phone bill and my electric bill."

"Well," said Root, "there's another one that I know of in Fort Kent called Wipe the Slate. I think they charge only $250. They're a private organization that apparently keyed into the Houlton computer."

"Private, or pirate?" asked Cass.

Cass received two phone calls the next day: the phone company and the electric company both warning him of shut-offs.

Cass offered to pay through Wipe the Slate, but both voices said no - government regulations.

"You can get away with paying off your credit cards through that organization, but not utilities," Cass was told.

Cass again said he could pay through Root's store, but was told certified agents only.

Eventually, his phone did not work, and two months later his lights would not go on. No phone. No electricity.

He emptied and cooked on his wood stove the perishables in his refrigerator, went to Root's and stocked up on canned food.

"I guess we'll just have to sit and wait for the tax collector," he told Sniper.

And that's what Cass did. He sat and waited. Sniper died of old age in September, 2031. Cass made a grave for him in the woods.

Things around him grew darker as his vision failed. With no electricity, Cass sat at night near the wood stove thinking of Isabel. Dreaming of hunting and fishing. Thinking of Isabel. Darker and darker grew Cass' world.

Later in 2031, too late, his son from Key Largo arrived. Bert found his father sitting by the wood stove - the fire had gone out.

"Dad, I brought you a computer," Bert said.

But Cass was dead. Strangely, he was smiling. He died in the darkness thinking of Isabel.

DAMAGE

Ellen, steaming coffee cup in hand, stared out the window into her backyard. She noticed that some sere leaves gathered on the outside window sill. The kids' swings seemed especially cold on this chill mid-November Maine day. She sensed the winter moving in like an unwanted guest.

Her two boys had been packed off to school. As she sipped her coffee, she thought of yesterday's phone call. Bill had left seven months ago. Seven months! Then he called yesterday wanting to meet the boys and her for Thanksgiving.

She had slammed the receiver. He called back.

Apologies, sorrow, missing her and the boys - she listened, her fury increasing.

"But you never told me where you've been," she said, struggling to keep her voice from screeching.

"I'll explain all that. Right now I know I can't be happy without you and the boys."

"What game are you playing? Have played? Still going on? A game you thought you won? Are winning? And now you want to come back."

She hung up.

Having finished her coffee, she had to face the rest of the day - alone - as usual -till the boys came home.

She studied her face in the mirror. She always considered herself pretty. Bill always made her feel that way. He always told her how beautiful she was.

Beautiful? At least pretty, she thought. She knew her assets - the blue eyes contrasted to her dark brown hair. At 27, she had a firm body. She knew men looked at her.

Bill had looked at her seven years ago. She had been walking to work when she stopped in a coffee shop. She was early, as usual. She had time to sit before walking two buildings away. She would still be early.

He boldly sat at her table, his smile, his flashing white teeth, his curly closely cropped hair. His brown eyes stared at her.

"You are the most beautiful woman I have ever seen."

She laughed.

"No, really," he said. "You have to meet me somewhere, sometime. You name it. You tell me."

That started it. She could not forget that day. She never would. And now it came flooding back, overwhelming her.

But then she thought of another day - seven years later - seven months ago: the day he left. He had left for work before she got up. She found a note:

"Ellen,

I'm not coming home anymore.

Bill"

No goodbye, no explanation, only that blunt note.

She was dazed. She called his work.

"He doesn't work here anymore," the woman said. "He left about two weeks ago."

Two weeks! He had been planning to leave her for two weeks. She never suspected. He treated her so well - always - even before he left - especially before he left. Maybe that special treatment was a sign.

She tried to trace him - unsuccessfully. She imagined many things - fantastic things. Maybe he was a spy for the CIA. Maybe he was kidnapped and forced to leave that message. More realistic: there was another woman.

She told the boys the truth: your father left. They cried for an explanation. Maybe he committed suicide, she thought. No, another woman.

Long days, expecting to hear, turned into longer nights. She ached for him. Never hearing.

And yesterday the phone call. There had been times that she

had actually forgotten about him - not exactly forgotten - but no longer expecting to hear from him.

With the phone call, all the inner turmoil returned. As the day went on, she knew she wanted him back, but she also knew that she could not take back such a deceitful man. But curiosity was gnawing away at her like a starving beast.

While she was awaiting the boys, the phone rang. It was Bill.

"Tell me the truth," she demanded. "Did you leave for another woman?"

There was a long silence. "Well?" she asked.

"Yes," he said hesitantly, "but it was all a mistake. I now know I can't be happy with her."

"Too bad." She hung up.

She wanted him back, but she could not have him.

She had been forced to return to work. Fortunately, Mr. Shaffer, her former employer, welcomed her back. When she explained to him, through tears she could not hold back, he arranged for her to work at home so that she could still care for her boys.

"In these days of the new-fangled technology, I can help you," he said.

She was ever so thankful to this man who was now in his sixties and only semi-literate with his computer. But Mr. Shaffer was smart enough to hire the brightest young people who knew all about computers.

So now Ellen did not need Bill, who seemed only to be looking out for number one.

He called back.

"I'll be over Thanksgiving, "he said, as bold as ever.

"No you won't. I have a restraining order against you." She did not, but she wanted him to think so. And if he did show up, she would call the police anyway.

"It's over," she said. "I have plans. Get it?"

"How about the day after?"

"Bill, don't you understand? I'm sure you do, but let me be clear. I never want to see you again. Now you say you want to come back, but the damage has been done."

She hung up. Even curiosity could not convince her to accept him back into what was now her home.

The door bell rang. When she opened the door, she noticed that the flakes were falling from the snow clouds that now filled the sky.

"Mr. Shaffer asked me to deliver this turkey," said a tall, blue-eyed man.

"Thank you," said Ellen. "Thank him for me."

The man stared at her. She looked back at him, noticed his eyes, his handsome face.

"You are absolutely beautiful," he said. "Please don't take

offense. I mean it sincerely. You are the most beautiful woman I have ever seen."

"Thank you for the compliment," said Ellen, "but I've heard that before."

And she quietly closed the door.

ENNUI
or
THE PORCH POTATO

Every day at 4 p.m. John Vandenhenden sits, with a glass of wine, on his front porch. From this second floor balcony he watches the traffic - mostly pedestrians - on side suburban street. The cars are very few, and they proceed slowly, cautiously, because of the walkers.

Five years ago John's parents were killed in an automobile accident. John's father was a big time investment broker, and John, an only child, inherited 22 million dollars. He promptly quit his job as an insurance salesman and ever since lived on the second floor of his two-family house. He had no interest in his work, rarely sold an insurance policy, and refused the downstairs tenants a lease renewal. No one has lived on the first floor since they vacated. John wanted it that way.

Not only had John no interest in his work, but he had no

interest in anything. He slept late, sat around till two p.m. when he ate lunch. Then he sat around, sometimes turning the television on, even though he had no interest in anything on the tube. When four o'clock came, he poured his glass of wine and sat on his porch till dark. He passively watched the strollers. Many of them walked their dogs.

John had no interest in any of the pedestrians, but he waved to them anyway. Most waved back: the elderly couples, the young men trying to keep in shape, the children - all waved. The young women did not wave. He wondered why.

Yes, he wondered why he never got along with females. As a teenager he had had a few dates, but the girls never accepted his request for a second date. Because he had no interest in anything, he never had anything to talk about. Some girls were interested in music, some in sports, some in the lives of famous actors, some in movies, some in their future.

"Which college are you going to?" he would be asked.

"None." End of conversation.

"What's your favorite baseball team?"

"I don't follow baseball."

"Who's your favorite singer?"

"I don't know."

On and on with these questions! No subject interested John.

Once Joe Prato, the closest person John could call a friend, arranged a date for John with a blonde bombshell. She was not all that beautiful, but she looked great in a tight sweater. She was slightly overweight, but just enough to make her look sexy. She also had a tarnished reputation. Joe thought that if anyone could bring out the personality of John Vandenhenden, Sally Macintosh could.

The date was a disaster. John and Sally went to the movies. On the way to the theater, John felt uncomfortable because Sally asked so many questions.

He was happy when they got to the movies and the film began. Though he had no interest in the film, at least he did not have to talk. Once during the film his hand brushed Sally's arm. She thought he was trying to hold her hand, so she gently grasped his hand. John thought he would die of embarrassment.

"I have to go to the bathroom," John whispered as he stumbled over the patrons in his row of seats.

After the movie John could not wait to get Sally home. He drove at breakneck speed, rushed through amber lights, and screeched to a halt in front of Sally's house.

"Good night," he said without getting out of the car, leaving Sally to her own devices.

"Aren't you going to kiss me good night?" she asked, leaning into John.

"No."

When Joe asked Sally how the date went, she said, "He's too intellectual for me."

This confirmed Joe's belief that Sally was not the brightest star in the heavens.

So John grew up without women - or men for that matter. He had no friends. After Joe went to college and eventually married, John never saw him again. John declined the invitation to Joe's wedding.

His wealthy father got John the job at the insurance agency. John was a complete failure at selling insurance, but the agency kept him on to please Mr. Vandenhenden.

Now John had no interest in ever leaving his house. He was content to watch the world go by. He hired a woman to do his food shopping, to do his laundry, and to keep the house clean. John hired her because she was a deaf mute. They communicated by writing notes. She came once a week at 11 a.m. and was done with whatever she had to do by noon. For one hour's work John paid her $500. He did not care about the money. He simply wanted everything taken care of, and Mrs. Kimmel, incapable of making small talk, did what he wanted and asked no questions. John liked it that way.

John was content. He enjoyed waving at people, and he liked when they waved back - though he had no interest in getting to know them. The little children coming home from school, carrying their school books or lunch boxes, or wearing back packs waved joyfully to the "strange man," as they called him. The teenagers enjoyed waving at John - some whispering that he was the "crazy man" of the neighborhood. The married couples and the senior citizens wondered about John, but they soon forgot him when they did not see him. A few had heard he was wealthy, but no one knew for sure.

Sipping his wine, John sat on the balcony day after day. He laughed at the dog walkers. The dogs were of all sizes - as were the walkers.

John developed a liking for a favorite dog and a favorite dog walker. He heard some of her teenage friends call the walker Melissa. And he heard Melissa call her tiny terrier Rupert.

"Rupert, don't go in the street. Rupert, run with me. Rupert, go in the house." Whatever command Melissa gave the dog, Rupert obeyed.

John waited patiently for Melissa to get home from school and walk Rupert. It was the first time John had an interest in anything.

John always waved at Melissa. Sometimes she waved back, hesitantly. Sometimes she did not.

The women in their twenties and thirties never returned John's wave. If they were with their husbands, the husbands waved. If alone or walking their dogs, they never waved. They looked straight ahead.

After dark John would watch television, but he found he was

not interested in anything. He would begin watching a movie, but fifteen minutes later he switched channels.

If he watched a sporting event, he never knew the score and never cared who won.

Whatever he watched - sitcoms, game shows, melodramas, detective dramas - he had no interest. He kept flicking the remote until complete boredom set in. He clicked off the television and went to bed. Before he fell asleep, he would think of Rupert. He kept picturing Melissa and her dog. He even thought he heard Melissa's voice: "Stay here, Rupert. Come by me, Rupert."

It always took him the longest time to fall asleep. Often, in the middle of the night, he would get up, but looking around the house, he knew he had nothing to do. He would eat. Having eaten, he was no longer tired. He would once again turn on the television, but after twenty minutes, he would turn it off.

On warm nights he would sit on the porch. An occasional car would go by, but no walkers, no dogs. He would see a cat slink across the road. After staring into the darkness, John would eventually shuffle off to bed. The morning would come, and he would repeat the routine of his day - looking forward to Melissa and Rupert.

Though he never weighed himself, John knew he must have gained forty pounds since he left the agency five years ago. He never exercised. He simply had no interest in keeping himself fit.

He was content when four o'clock arrived. He sat on his porch, sipping his wine, watching the activity.

There goes Mrs. Finch with her shaggy dog. He had overheard someone say the Mr. Finch had died. John remembered Mr. Finch because sometimes Mr. Finch would walk the dog.

Here come Billy and Milly with their poodle. He did not know their names, but he called them Billy and Milly.

Then there were Mel 'n' Collie. The dog certainly was a collie, but John did not know Mel's real name.

And then there were Melissa and Rupert. John waved. Melissa hesitantly waved back.

It was the end of summer. The days were becoming shorter. At dusk the walkers were few. Melissa brought Rupert out for his final walk of the day.

"Rupert, stay on the sidewalk," Melissa said as she tugged at the leash forcing the dog out of the road.

Suddenly, John saw a convertible speeding down the road. Three teenagers were singing at the top of their drunken voices. Melissa pulled the leash again to make sure Rupert was on the sidewalk.

As the car sped by, Rupert began barking and ran at the car. Melissa held the leash tightly, but the leash snapped. Rupert ran head first into the side of the car. The dog's bark turned into a yelp, and John saw Rupert bounce off the car and land at Melissa's feet as the car disappeared heading out of town.

John ran down the stairs, ran to Melissa. Before he got there, a small crowd had already gathered. They must have heard Melissa's scream. She was now crying uncontrollably, kneeling next to the lifeless Rupert.

John knelt too. He stroked Rupert's head.

"Poor Rupert."

He reached out to hug Melissa.

"Don't touch me, you pervert. Don't touch my dog. My dog is dead." Her sobbing continued.

"But I love Rupert," John said.

"No you don't. You're nothing but a pervert. Everybody knows that. Get away from me. Go back up on your porch where you belong, pervert!"

Two people from the crowd, their arms around Melissa, led her away. Police had arrived to take the dog away. They asked if anyone had seen the license plate on the car - if anyone knew the boys in the car. No one had.

As the crowd dispersed, John got up from his knees and shuffled across the street back to his house. It was the first time in four years that he had left his house. And now he would return determined never to leave again. He was sure that this house would be where he would die.

Automobiles had taken from him his only interests in life: his parents and Melissa and Rupert.

He made his way back to the porch. His wine was still on the table next to his chair. He sat and sipped.

"Poor Rupert - poor Melissa." The sun had gone down.

"I'm not a pervert, Mama," he said into the darkness

A tear trickled down his cheek.

HATRED

"...now could I drink hot blood, And do such bitter business as the day Would quake to look on." - Shakespeare

At three o'clock every morning, I awake with the urge to kill.

Fortunately, I fall back to sleep after about an hour and awake at eight with the thought of murder buried.

Hatred! It rises to my conscious self every morning - in the dark depths of night. Hatred! For who?

My wife Thelma? Why did I ever marry someone named Thelma? Why did I ever marry?

I know she was unfaithful to me.

Hatred! For Carlo Fortunetti. He's the one.

One day I had taken a day off. It would not be unusual for Carlo to visit in the evening. We had grown up together. Graduated high school the same year.

But to visit in the middle of the day!

Carlo walked in. I was standing at the top of the stairs. When he saw me, he took the fatal step backwards. It was automatic. It was his instinct to leave.

But he recovered.

"I saw your car and thought I'd stop. Are you ill?"

Plausible! Plausible!

But that backward step – a slight second in time – sealed his doom.

Hatred! For Bill Green – my supervisor. He passed me over and promoted someone else.

I remember having to read "Othello" when I was a senior in high school. I loved Iago.

I remember Miss Hinch, my English teacher, saying that there wasn't enough motivation for Iago to be as evil as he was. She pointed out that scholars said (she was very fair to give credit to scholars, but I always thought it was a way of bragging that she read all about the authors we studied) – well, she said that the scholars said that even though Iago tells us that Othello made Cassio lieutenant instead of Iago, that wasn't enough motivation to have Iago do the evil deeds that he does.

Well, Miss Hinch and all you scholars, I assume you haven't been passed over for promotion.

I understand Iago; therefore, Bill Green must go.

Hatred! For Mary Simms.

She works in the office. She thinks she's hot shit just because she has a tight little ass that wiggles extemporaneously. She doesn't like that I call her Mary Canary. And when I grabbed her ass, she went running to Bill Green crying sexual harassment. Sexual harassment! If I ever caught her alone in the warehouse, I'd show her what sexual harassment really is.

So she went running to Bill Green, who she was probably having sex with, and got me put on probation at work.

"If it ever happens again," Green said, "you will be fired."

I wanted to grab his flabby chin and make it impossible for him to swallow.

But it wasn't three a.m., so I put my tail between my legs and trudged out of his office.

Hatred! For Bixby Evans.

Bixby, the bastard, thinks he knows everything. Any time anyone brings up a subject, Bixby begins pontificating on that subject. You can't shut him up. Someday I'll cut his tongue out before I bash his brains in.

But now it's eight a.m. and all my murderous intentions have subsided. Now I have to face the drudgery of work at the warehouse. Bring the stock in B12 to men's wear, in G6 to appliances. Unpack the deliveries. On and on – me! Still a stock boy and know-it-all Bixby (he's the one promoted instead of me) bragging about how good the Pittsburgh Penguins are.

I didn't need Bixby's love of the Penguins to make me hate the Penguins. Hatred! I know what Bixby doesn't know. The

Penguins cheated in the draft this year when this hotshot that everyone wanted was drafted. Everyone wanted him, the baby-faced phenom.

Well, that year of the draft, Pittsburgh won the lottery for the number one pick. They finished among the worst in the league, not the very worst, but bad enough to be in the lottery. The lottery is weighted so that the worse the team, the better chance it has to win that coveted number-one choice. Pittsburgh did not have the best chance of winning the lottery.

The Pittsburgh franchise was in bad shape. They were even talking about moving to some God-forsaken place like Winnipeg or who remembers now, like Paducah, Kentucky.

Now get this: before the draft, The Hockey News reported that young hot shot was working out with the Penguins. And what happens? Pittsburgh wins the draft lottery, getting the number one pick, saving the franchise for Pittsburgh.

What is amazing to me is that apparently no one put two and two together – or if anyone did, he was silenced. This unbelievable coincidence eventually led to a Stanley Cup – not right away, but eventually.

Why do I know this and nobody else does?

Hatred! The Pittsburgh Penguins, the National Hockey League. A couple of bombs in the right place will take care of the Pittsburgh franchise and cripple the NHL.

But see – now Bixby is making me think that it's three a.m.

Bixby likes the Pirates and the Steelers, too. I used to like the Pirates, but now I don't because of Bixby. He can really ruin a man's life.

I never like the Steelers, especially when they had that quarterback. He even tried to sing country music. Some people can't be satisfied to stick to one line of work. Now he is a TV commentator, yapping away like Bixby.

So now I'm handed instructions by Bixby – a blond, blue-eyed lover boy (in love with that hot shot hockey player. Bixby knows everything). I can't wait to amputate his tongue. I can feel it in my hand.

Three a.m. – I'm awake. My bedroom is dimly lit by a night light, but I can see Thelma's white neck. It seems so inviting, just waiting, begging to have it slashed. I imagine I can see the bright red blood flowing, draining the life out of her.

"Go back to sleep," I tell myself.

The next thing I know I was being awakened by a stranger in some kind of uniform – white. I wasn't in my bed. I was lying on my back. When I tried to move, I was strapped in.

This stranger put handcuffs on my wrists and ankles, and then unstrapped me and made me sit up.

"Your lawyer is here to see you," the stranger said. A lawyer? For what? In came an impeccably dressed, impeccably groomed man. Apparently he is the lawyer.

"The only possible plea you can make to save your life is an insanity plea."

I stared at him.

"Do you understand?" he said irritably.

"No."

"If you want to have any chance to saving your life, you have to accept my advice. I'll make the insanity plea. All you have to say is not guilty.

"Not guilty for what?"

"Look," he said with an air of disgust, "don't play games with me. I've been assigned this case by the court. You have to be insane to go on the murder rampage that you did. I'll be able to get you incarcerated in a hospital for the criminally insane. Probably for life. The other alternative is the death penalty – which you might get anyway if the prosecutor can prove you knew what you were doing."

"What did I do?"

"Look, I don't have time to tell you what you already know. And if you don't know, then it makes your plea easily provable." And he left.

I was transported to a cell. A cot, a sink, a toilet – nothing else. Every now and then someone would push a tray through a slot in the door. I had no awareness of time. When the lights went out, I slept. When they came on, I sat staring at the walls.

I had no idea of time, but strangely, I never woke up in the darkness with the urge to kill. I felt I was being rehabilitated. But I truly didn't know why I was here.

One day – I guess it was a day because the lights were on, the tray, in addition to food, had a newspaper on it. It was one of those supermarket sensational rags that had outlandish stories like "man born with wings," "ravens really do talk," "four-headed elephant seen in the Congo," and other such trash.

In this one, on the front page, the headline ready, "Lunatic on a Murder Spree," and there was a photo of a man in handcuffs being escorted to jail. Strangely, the man looked familiar.

As I read the story, I knew everyone involved except the murderer that the police mentioned. There it was! Someone had killed my wife. The murderer slit her throat while she was in bed. It must have been Carlo. Who else would she have been in bed with?

But wait – here was Mary Canary. They found her remains in the warehouse. She was sexually abused, her breasts cut off – cause of death: strangulation.

And Bill Green – a knife in his neck. And – how horrible – Bixby with his tongue severed, his blue eyes cut out, and his skull bashed in.

And, finally Carlo. So maybe he didn't kill Thelma. They found Carlo in the parking lot of a local tavern, his torso cut from the lower stomach to the breast bone. The murderer had cut open Carlo's jeans and castrated him.

Wait! Wait! I'm recalling something. The fatal backward step. It happened again when he saw my Bowie knife. He took that fatal backward step – the last step he ever took.

So, I must have been involved. The murderer's name, as I re-read the beginning, is Vance Pilfred. I'm trying very hard to remember if that's my name.

Well, life has become peaceful. The trial was tedious and most of the time I didn't know what they were talking about. I didn't get to say much. I really didn't want to because I didn't know what happened – except what I read in that newspaper. They kept referring to me as Mr. Pilfred – so I guess that's my name.

Day by day passes. I have no sense of time. The nice people take good care of me. I don't have to think about anything.

Every once in a while I meet with this nice lady. She says she is a doctor who is trying to help me, but I don't understand. I don't feel sick.

Being here makes me love everybody. They're so nice. I sleep soundly every night. I don't wake up with hatred.

There's only one thing I think about: Once I get out of here. I have to take care of the Penguins and the NHL.

WHERE'S CHIPPER?

Duane Morton met Chipper at the Roadside Diner, just off Straightaway Road near Rural Route 2.

Chipper was waiting on the counter customers. Duane always sat at the counter because he always ate alone. Duane was wearing a red tee shirt that contrasted with his green eyes.

"You look rather chipper tonight," the waitress said to him as she poured his coffee.

Duane laughed.

As he was leaving, Duane said, "Goodbye, Chipper."

"Goodbye, Chipper," she responded.

Whenever Duane returned to the diner, the two always called each other Chipper.

Chipper was a 30-year-old brunette with bluish gray eyes. She had a compact body on a five foot four frame. She had what men called a killer smile. While working, she always tied her hair in a pink ribbon.

Duane was pudgy, six two, with black hair. Though he tried to keep clean shaved, his facial hair grew so fast that he appeared to always need a shave.

One night when Duane arrived at the diner, Chipper was not there. He was surprised that he felt so sullen while being served by another waitress.

As he left, Duane saw Chipper outside smoking a cigarette. "Hey, Chipper," he said, "are you going or coming?"

"I wish I was going, but I have to work till midnight tonight."

"Too bad."

That night at midnight Duane pulled up in the diner's parking lot. Five minutes later, Chipper emerged from the diner.

"Hey, Chipper. Can we have a drink together?" She hesitated, but agreed. "I'll follow you," she said.

Duane drove to Bilbo's Pub. He constantly looked in the rear view mirror to be sure Chipper was still following. He had been surprised that she agreed to the drink. Women usually did not take up Duane on his offers. He was not sure she would actually follow him. Duane interpreted that driving in separate cars meant a drink and nothing else.

Duane introduced Chipper to the bartender Hylo Brown.

"What is this heavenly vision I see before me? Hast thou stepped down from thy heavenly throne?"

Chipper laughed.

"Hylo has a Ph. D. so he talks different than the rest of us."

"Ah, yes," said Hylo, "the injustice of this society that forces so educated a man to be servile to the masses. So, what paradisal nectar can I get you, my angelic sylph?"

Chipper was not sure what to order.

"May I suggest an ambrosia of my own mixing?"

"Sure," said Chipper.

"I'll have the same," said Duane.

Hylo put two mixtures on the bar.

"A drink suitable for both a decadent man and a goddess."

Duane sipped the drink.

"Cut the shit, Hylo. This is a rum and coke."

"Ah, to denigrate the nectar concocted by a doctor of mixology is blasphemous."

Chipper laughed. "It tastes good," she said.

"This heavenly creature knows ambrosia," said Hylo.

Hylo felt he had performed enough for this newcomer named Chipper. He waited on other customers.

While Chipper and Duane conversed, an elderly couple came from a table to talk to Duane.

"I am so glad to see you here with this beautiful decent woman," said the elderly woman. She slurred her words.

Despite his embarrassment, Duane thanked her.

The elderly man and the elderly woman stumbled out.

Chipper laughed.

"That was my old Sunday school teacher," Duane said.

"They seem a couple made for each other," said Chipper.

"They never married. He's the deacon at the Presbyterian Church. Both of them come in here every night and drink themselves silly. Often they're already drunk when they come in."

"Sex before or after or both?" asked Chipper.

"What a horrid thought," said Duane. "I can't imagine them having sex - though I guess they've been shacking up for years."

"More drinks?" It was Hylo.

"No," said Chipper.

"Not yet," said Duane.

"I'll not lead you into temptation," said Hylo.

"He's good at pushing drinks," Duane said.

"Are you usually in here with indecent women?" asked Chipper.

"Old lady Crankshaft has a way of putting me down - ever since Sunday school. You know, I thought she was an old witch then. How old must she be now?"

"Well, what about the indecent women?"

"Well, I'm not a virgin, but I don't chase after indecent women."

"They don't need chasing. They're always available."

"More drinks?" Hylo again.

"No," said Chipper.

"Yes," said Duane. "Let's talk about you."

"I prefer to remain your mystery woman," said Chipper as she untied her pink ribbon. Her light brown hair tumbled down to her shoulders.

Duane looked into her blue-gray eyes.

"I've never seen anyone so beautiful." He meant it.

"Right! That's what you tell them all." She smiled the killer smile.

Duane was completely smitten.

"I think I love you."

Chipper laughed.

"The goddess has let down her hair." It was Hylo with Duane's second drink. "May I tempt you further, you beautiful creature. Another drink?"

"No," said Chipper. "It's time to go."

Duane quickly drained his glass and accompanied Chipper to her car.

"A souvenir," she said, as she put the pink ribbon in his hand.

Two days later when Duane returned to the diner, Chipper was not there. He assumed she was working late.

He returned at midnight. Two waitresses came out, got into their cars, and drove away.

No chipper.

Duane went into the diner, but the waitresses were not Chipper.

"Her day off," he assumed.

The next evening at the diner - no Chipper.

The next evening Duane asked the gray-haired grouchy waitress, "Where's Chipper?"

"Who the hell is Chipper?"

"The woman who usually works this counter."

"I usually work this counter," Miss Congeniality snapped at him.

Duane asked the cashier.

"Who's Chipper?" was again the response.

Duane sought out the manager.

"Who's Chipper?"

"The woman with the blue-gray eyes."

The manager stroked his chin.

After about twenty seconds, which seemed like an eternity to Duane, the manager said, "You must mean the girl who just quit a few days ago."

"Quit!"

"Yes. She didn't even give us notice. Just came in and said she quit."

"Where did she go?"

"I don't know."

Duane was confused.

"But her name wasn't Chipper," the manager said.

"Well, what is her name?"

"Hope something."

"Can you tell me her full name?"

"I don't know if I should."

"Please." Duane was desperate.

"I'll have to look." The manager went into his office.

Duane stopped another waitress.

"Where does Hope live?"

"Damned if I know," she said.

The manager returned. "Hope Alloway."

"Do you have her address?"

"I can't give you that," said the manager.

Duane offered him a twenty dollar bill.

"Sorry," said the manager, "I can't. It could cost me my job."

Frustrated, Duane left. Outside a waitress came up to him.

"I know you and Hope got along together," she said. "I don't know her address, but I think she lives somewhere out on Freedom Road."

"Thanks, thanks," Duane said touching her shoulder.

"I could use the twenty," she said.

"Oh, sure, sure." Duane gave her the twenty dollar bill.

Driving out Freedom Road, Duane saw no houses. It was a heavily wooded area. The sun had gone down. It was a cloudy night. Sporadically the full moon would peek through the clouds.

He stopped the car, got out, and shouted: "Chi-i-ipper! Where are you? Where's Chipper?"

He drove into the darkness for almost five miles. He finally spotted a house behind several trees. There was a long driveway.

"What the hell!" He decided to drive up to the front door.

The house was rather dilapidated. He wondered if it had been abandoned.

Wondering what he would find, he clanked the heavy knocker.

An outside light came on.

Someone cracked the door open and peered out from behind a chain.

"Hello," said Duane.

The door closed. Duane heard the chain being removed. The door opened.

"Come in, my good man," said a kindly voice.

Duane's jaw dropped when he recognized Reverend Brown, the minister of the Presbyterian Church.

"What brings you out to my wilderness home?" asked the benevolent minister.

Duane entered.

"I always thought you lived in the house next to the church."

"I do, but I prefer this isolation during the week so that I can contemplate and prepare my Sunday sermons."

The reverend led Duane into a well-furnished living room.

"Please sit. May I get you some refreshment?" asked the kindly minister. "I trust that you have been staying away from my brother Hylo. He serves the devil's drink."

Duane sat, but refused refreshment.

"So - you haven't told me what brings you here."

"Well," said Duane, "I'm a little embarrassed to say." He hesitated. "I'm looking for a woman."

The reverend laughed. "Any woman, or someone in particular?"

Duane smiled. "No, not any woman. I wonder if you know where Hope Alloway lives."

"Ah, yes, that beautiful woman of the pink ribbon. Many men have sought her, but it seems she hasn't been interested in any of them."

"She's probably not interested in me either, but I'd like to see her. She just disappeared from her job at the diner."

"It is her tendency to disappear," said Reverend Brown. "I wasn't aware that she was employed at the diner."

"Well she isn't anymore."

There was prolonged silence.

"Are you able to tell me where she lives?" Duane finally asked.

"Of course, of course. She lives down the road about two miles. Like my house, hers is set back in the woods. You may not be able to see it. Maybe you should try tomorrow in the daylight."

Duane got up to leave.

"And, oh, stay away from my brother Hylo and Bilbo's Pub."

Back in his car, Duane thought," I can't wait till tomorrow. There's something drawing me to her."

Watching his speedometer to determine that he went two miles, Duane saw a house as he pulled around a curve. How could he not see it? The house was bathed in light. It seemed like daylight.

As he touched the knocker, the door moved. It was open, unlocked. Chipper was lying on a divan. She was dressed (hardly) in a sheer negligee. Nothing was said. She reached for him. He threw himself in her arms.

Duane had never experienced anything like his sexual encounter with Chipper. He needed Hylo Brown's vocabulary to describe it. He swore he heard the music of the spheres. What he felt was beyond an earthly feeling.

It was well after midnight when he stopped at Bilbo's. Certainly he needed a drink.

Hylo was not the bartender.

Duane ordered a shot of whiskey with a beer chaser.

"Where's Hylo?"

Duane had never been in the pub when Hylo was not there.

"Dunno. I'm new here. Just hired."

That night Duane slept a heavenly sleep.

After work the next day, Duane decided to eat at the diner.

He had not been there for the last two nights. He had opted for Burger King.

He was surprised to be greeted by Hylo. "What are you doing here?" Duane asked.

"I have become the new proprietor of this respectable establishment. I have forsaken the sinful past of the pub."

Duane laughed. "I can't believe it."

"Do believe. I have hired someone that you have known." He pointed to the waitress behind the counter. She had her back to them while she was writing a bill for a patron. Her brown hair was tied up in a pink ribbon.

Duane rushed to the counter.

The waitress turned around. She was Miss Crankshaft.

"Aaaaaaaaaaa!" Duane's scream could be heard throughout the diner. Patrons and waitresses turned to see.

"What's wrong?" asked Miss Crankshaft with a sneer. "Go to hell, you shithead. I've never liked you since you were ten years old."

Duane ran toward the door. He was stopped by the Deacon.

"You have to pay," said the Deacon.

"I didn't buy any food," said Duane.

"You have to pay - for your sins."

"As you can see," said Hylo, "I have surrounded myself with old friends."

"You must pay," the Deacon repeated.

"Let him go," said Hylo. "He is already in the process of paying."

"Where's Chipper? Is she here too?"

"Chipper?"

"Yes. Chipper. You know. The woman I was with the other night."

"Ah," said Hylo, "that pultritudenous hunk of goddess flesh."

"Where is she?"

"Certainly not here," said Hylo.

As Duane broke away from the Deacon, Hylo shouted after him, "You never know who will be wearing the pink ribbons."

He jumped in his car and drove out to Freedom Road. He couldn't find Chipper's house. He stopped where he thought it had been, stood in the middle of the forest, and shouted:

"Chi-i-i-perrr! Where are you?"

He found Reverend Brown's house, but there was no response when Duane continued slamming the knocker till his hand was bloody. He noticed some hair growing in his palm. The hairs on his arms and the backs of his hands were thicker than usual.

He drove into town and knocked at Reverend Brown's house next to the church. The minister's assistant opened the door.

Duane saw Reverend Brown down the hall.

"Where is she?"

"Come in, my good man. Calm yourself. Where is who?"

The minister led Duane to a chair.

"WHO? Chipper! Where's Chipper?"

"Who is Chipper?"

"You know. The woman you directed me to."

"I don't understand."

"Last night!"

"Last night?"

"I was at your house on Freedom Road! Look what she's done to me." Duane held out his hands.

The good clergyman took Duane's hands, saw dried blood.

"What is it, my son? Let me wash the blood."

"Not the blood! The hair! The hair! The growths of hair!"

"My son, we all have some hair growing on the hands and arms." Reverend Brown showed Duane the backs of his hands and arms.

"But not this much!"

"I daresay, my hair is thinner than yours."

Duane shook his head.

"I believe we should call Dr. Elmer."

Duane bolted out of the house.

As days passed, Duane's stubble grew into a beard. When he shaved, he could not get down to his skin. The facial hair was too thick.

He discovered lycanthropy on his computer.

Back to the diner, he sought Hylo.

"Hylo, you have to help me. Look what Chipper has done to me."

"What?" asked Hylo.

"The hair! Look at my beard, my hands, my arms!"

Hylo saw nothing unusual.

"You've always had a thick beard when you let it grow more than a day. It's a sign of a man's virility. You're not a boy. You're a man!"

There was no help. No one saw the hair as anything unusual but Duane himself. He was convinced it was all Chipper's fault.

He had to find her.

He drove to the house where he was convinced he met Reverend Brown. He was determined to walk the area from Brown's house to where he would inevitably come to Chipper's house.

He walked for more than an hour. Sweat soaked him. His palms had hair sprouting. His arms were thick with hair soaked in sweat. His beard was thicker than ever.

"Chi-i-i-pperrr! Where are you?"

After walking what he was sure was more than two miles, he sat on a log - a dead tree. He saw at the edge of a clearing a tree with a pink ribbon hanging from its branch.

Despite his aching muscles, Duane ran to the clearing.

They were all there: Hylo, Reverend Brown, the Deacon, Miss Crankshaft, and - he could not believe his eyes -Chipper. Her arms were extended toward him.

"All of you! Get rid of this hair! Help me!"

They were all smiling.

He went toward Chipper. In her hand was a tube.

"Here, my love," she whispered. "Put this at your heart. My love will penetrate. It will free you of the hair." She smiled her killer smile.

Duane followed instructions and felt the explosion throughout his body. Then he felt nothing.

First, they found the car next to an abandoned house. They searched for two more days before they found his lifeless body in the woods.

"He was a happy man," Reverend Brown said, "but something had gone wrong. He imagined that hair was growing all over his body."

"And he seemed to have an obsession for someone named Chipper," said Hylo Brown.

"A strange suicide, pointing the revolver directly at his heart," said the minister.

"The autopsy showed he died from the silver bullet they found in his heart," said Hylo.

"I always knew there was something wrong with him -

ever since he was ten years old. I understand he was studying lycanthropy," said Miss Crankshaft.

"He imagined himself turning into a werewolf," said Dr. Elmer. "He was completely delusional. There are the old folklore myths of werewolves, but there is a psychological condition called medical lycanthropy. The individual believes he is becoming a wolf. He imagines his hair is growing excessively, or, amazing as it sounds, begins growing hair on the palms of his hands. The actual hair growth is very rare. Usually, as in Duane's case, the individual imagines hair growth."

"He always had a thick beard," said Miss Crankshaft. "But nothing unusual - nothing excessive," said Dr. Elmer.

"He said he had excessive hair, but when he showed me, there was nothing unusual," said Hylo. "How could all this happen?"

There was a shaking of heads, but no one had an answer except the Deacon: "He was paying for his sins."

They all toasted his memory. Even Reverend Brown had a drink of Hylo's mixture. "Here's to Duane Morton," said Reverand Brown. "He was a good man."

Charlie Casco stopped at the Roadside Diner just off Straightaway Road near Rural Route 2. Charlie was wearing a blue tee shirt that emphasized his blue eyes.

"You look rather chipper tonight," the waitress said as she poured his coffee and blinked her bluish-gray eyes and smiled her killer smile.

KRISTI, THE BARMAID

The pale man sipping on a Bud sat at the end of the bar. He had been sitting there since eight, and now it was past one.

"Christ! Three beers! He nursed three beers all night!" Kristi thought.

There were only three patrons in the bar. It was Tuesday on a side street bar in Atlanta, far from the fashionable clubs and restaurants.

"Tuesday nights are always slow," Kristi thought, "but this is ridiculous." She would not make much money tonight.

At the other end of the bar were two lovers. They sat close, often touching each other. "Definitely lovers," Kristi thought. "Married couples don't act like that." He ordered another Dewars on the rocks. She did not want another drink.

Hank, the cook, was sleeping in the kitchen. No one had ordered food since seven o'clock.

Kristi, with a smile, asked the pale man if he wanted another beer. He said okay.

Kristi had a great smile. She was harshly pretty - 37 with dark red hair. There were some lines developing around her eyes. She was dressed in jeans and a low cut blue blouse, showing off her still firm breasts. She knew the kind of blouse, cut just right, to please the men. Then there was her dynamite smile that brought out her inner beauty.

She had been married once when she was twenty-three, but it lasted only a year. It was unpleasant, so she never married again, preferring to befriend men for short periods of time with long intervals between. She was now in the midst of one of those long intervals.

The lovers left. There was a two-dollar tip on the bar.

"Damn," she said, a little louder than she meant to. The pale man heard her and smiled. He made a cell phone call. Apparently no one answered because he clicked off right away. He had been making calls all night, with the same result.

She hoped he would leave so that she could leave a little earlier than two.

She asked if he wanted another beer.

He declined.

"You know," he told her, "I always liked Atlanta till this morning."

"Why's that?"

"I woke up alone and cold."

"Must have been the air conditioning because it's damned hot. Been hot day and night all week."

"Cold inside. Cold and empty inside."

Kristi was used to hearing sad stories. She felt another coming on.

"You know, it's my birthday. At least it was till midnight."

"Happy birthday," she said sincerely.

"Not really. It's been the loneliest birthday of my life." There were tears in his eyes.

"Sorry." She didn't know what else to say. Despite her harsh look, Kristi had a sympathetic heart. She felt sorry, but wondered how she got into this conversation.

She scrutinized him more carefully. His bland, pale face contained two big brown eyes, sad eyes. They reminded Kristi of the eyes of a hound dog she once had.

He had a decent slim body. His hands were beautiful, long delicate fingers, the fingers of a surgeon or a musician.

"I've been calling her on the phone, but she doesn't answer. Somehow I have the feeling she's there."

Kristi knew "she" was the reason he was here on the bar stool sipping on his beer.

"You know, she used to pay attention to my birthday, but it seems this year she don't even care."

"Oh, brother!" Kristi thought.

"Is that the original spelling of your name or did you change it?" He was staring at her name tag on the low cut blouse.

Kristi was happy to change the subject.

"My mother named me Catherine, but I thought Kristi was sexier."

"It is. What's your last name?"

"Fox."

"Wow! Kristi Fox - that's a hot name."

Kristi never gave her real last name. "Fox is good enough," she thought.

It was nearly two o'clock.

"Hank, wake up," Kristi called into the kitchen. "Closing time."

She grabbed a cloth and began wiping the counter.

"You have time for one more beer," she told pale face.

"OK," he said, pushing his glass toward her. "But I've got nowhere to go but this lonely hotel room where all I'll do is watch television till I fall asleep."

Kristi did not respond. She gave him a fresh beer. He made another phone call. Same result.

"Hey, Kristi Fox," he said, "I've never done what I'm going to do. It will sound like a line, but it is sincere."

She continued to wipe the bar.

"Come back with me to my room. Not for sex, but just to watch television with me and have conversation."

"Ha! It certainly sounds like a line," she said.

"It's not. I'm just lonely as hell."

He was so pathetic and looked so unhappy that Kristi believed him.

"Look," she said as sympathetically, but firmly, as she could. "I have another job that I have to be at at ten in the morning. I've got to get home and get some sleep. I'm truly sorry for your breakup with your girlfriend, wife, whatever, but I've got to get home."

He hung his head.

"He looks like such a loser," she thought.

He gulped down the beer. "Where do you work?"

"Kohl's."

He drew a card from his wallet. He wrote his room number on the back of it and pushed it toward her.

"In case you change your mind." He put money on the counter and left.

Kristi felt sad, but his request was truly outlandish.

When she picked up the money, she saw he left a fifty dollar tip.

She wanted to thank him, but he disappeared into the fog that had crept into Atlanta. She turned over the card. It read: "Philip Braxton, occulist. Have you had your eyes examined lately?" It gave his business address and phone number in Roswell.

She folded the fifty dollar bill around the card and slipped them into her purse. "Poor bastard," she said. "Well, at least he is financially well off." "What's that?" asked Hank, bleary-eyed, coming out of the kitchen. "Nothing. Just talking to myself. This job will do that to a person."

On her way home, driving through the fog, Kristi stopped at the all night supermarket and spent fifty dollars on much needed groceries.

When she arrived home, she looked at the business card again. She had lied about the morning job. She felt he was such a loser that she did not want to take up his offer. Besides, she did not believe the part about no sex.

She dropped the card in the trash.

"He just didn't turn me on," she thought. "That's what it came down to. Not the fifty. He just didn't turn me on."

She went to the kitchen cabinet, found the bottle of Jack Daniel's, cracked it open and poured herself a neat drink - an eight-ounce glass.

She turned the television on, found an old movie. It was "Cape Fear" with Gregory Peck and Robert Mitchum.

She took a deep drink and settled back on the couch. She planned to watch television till she fell asleep.

BURNT TOAST

"The toast has burnt edges," he bellowed. "I'll make you more," she said.

"No, damn it. You waste bread. I work my ass off and you can't even make toast. I'll eat this. Don't waste bread."

She remained silent, sitting with him at the table while he slurped his dunked bread in his coffee.

"Coffee's weak," he muttered.

Finally, he slammed the cup and stormed off to work.

She knew he worked hard in his construction job. He was now 51 and the physicality of his work was getting to him.

His exceptional strength made him the workhorse of the company, but now the aches kept increasing. She knew his back bothered him constantly.

She had grown numb to his criticism of her. She accepted it silently - actually afraid to complain. She was thankful that he never hit her. She no longer expected a compliment.

She remembered once before they were married that he told her she looked pretty in her new dress. Now she can't remember when she bought herself a new dress. She had to constantly order work clothes from the Duluth Trading Company catalogue. Food and his work clothes took up most of his paycheck.

They never went anywhere. Nights and weekends were spent with him watching television - actually his dozing in front of the television during a baseball game in summer and a football game in winter.

"Today's athletes can't compare to the athletes of the past," he complained.

She wondered how he could tell because he slept through most of the games. She knew he worked hard -physically hard. She felt sorry for him. He never moved up in the company. He was too valuable as the workhorse.

She loved him once, but she didn't think she loved him anymore. She felt sorry for him.

She often looked at herself in the mirror. Her hair had begun to gray. The lines in her face made her look 55 instead of 45. She had grown thin - almost shapeless. The men didn't look at her anymore. They used to, she remembered, when she had a nice figure and a youthful, pretty face. Others always told her husband that he robbed the cradle because when they married, she was 21 but looked 15. The years have caught up with her because she looked older than her husband now.

Sorrow was her way of life. Often she cried when trying to sleep. She cried silently so as not to wake him, while he snored and emitted a beer breath that permeated the room.

"Maybe if we would have had children, things would have been different," she thought. "But then, again, maybe he would have made the children as miserable as I am. Well," she thought, "at least when they grew up they could run away. Why can't I? No one would want me. I couldn't get a job." And then she tried to stop thinking, lapsing into her numbness.

Numbness had been her refuge.

He always expected dinner at four when he came home.

"I work my ass off. I'm starved at four. Make sure I don't have to wait."

His dinner was ready every day though he always found something to complain about. She silently nibbled at her food. His complaints were deflected by her numbness.

When he came home, his food was prepared for him and set at his normal place, but she wasn't sitting at the table waiting for him.

"This steak isn't cooked enough! It's getting cold." But he ate anyway.

He never understood where she got the pills.

He never understood how numbness became her escape.

And now she retreated into that numbness - forever.